D0975107

Jan 18

This book belongs to

....

Princess Pistachio
and Maurice the Magnificent

Marie-Louise Gay

pajamapress

Canada Council   Conseil des arts
for the Arts   du Canada

 **ONTARIO ARTS COUNCIL**
CONSEIL DES ARTS DE L'ONTARIO
an Ontario government agency
un organisme du gouvernement de l'Ontario

 Canadä

The publisher gratefully acknowledges the support of the Canada Council for the Arts and the Ontario Arts Council for its publishing program. We acknowledge the financial support of the Government of Canada through the Canada Book Fund (CBF) for our publishing activities.

Library and Archives Canada Cataloguing in Publication

Gay, Marie-Louise, author, illustrator
      Princess Pistachio and Maurice the magnificent
/ Marie-Louise Gay.
ISBN 978-1-77278-021-5 (hardback)
      I. Title.
PS8563.A868P75 2017   jC813'.54   C2016-906108-6

Publisher Cataloging-in-Publication Data (U.S.)

Names: Gay, Marie-Louise, author.
Title: Princess Pistachio and Maurice the Magnificent / Marie-Louise Gay.
Description: Toronto, Ontario, Canada: Pajama Press, 2016. | Summary: "When Pistachio's dog earns a starring role in a play, she can't talk about anything else for months. But the fame and fun cause trouble when Pistachio's best friend Madeline starts to feel left out" — Provided by publisher.
Identifiers: ISBN 978-1-77278-021-5 (paperback)
Subjects: LCSH: Dogs – Juvenile fiction. | Friendship – Juvenile fiction. | BISAC: JUVENILE FICTION / Readers / Chapter Books. | JUVENILE FICTION / Humorous Stories. | JUVENILE FICTION / Social Themes / Friendship.
Classification: LCC PZ7.G39Pr |DDC [E] – dc23

Original art created with India ink, watercolor, ink, and colored pencils.
Designed by Rebecca Bender

Manufactured by Friesens
Printed in Canada

Pajama Press Inc.
181 Carlaw Ave. Suite 207 Toronto, Ontario Canada, M4M 2S1

Distributed in Canada by UTP Distribution
5201 Dufferin Street Toronto, Ontario Canada, M3H 5T8

Distributed in the U.S. by Ingram Publisher Services
1 Ingram Blvd. La Vergne, TN 37086, USA

For Jacob

· Chapter 1 ·
A Dog's Life

Princess Pistachio's dog is sleeping belly-up on his favorite plaid cushion. He is snoring like a frog with a cold. Every few seconds, his short legs spin frantically in the air as if he were swimming upside down. He whimpers and drools.

I wonder what he dreams about, thinks Pistachio. *Running after squirrels? Being a superhero? Winning a dog marathon?*

Her dog sleeps most of the day. Then he sleeps most of the night. In between naps, he eats.

A dog's life is really boring, thinks Pistachio. *Poor Dog. He needs adventure and excitement in his life.*

"Dog, let's go for a walk," says Pistachio. "A nice long walk in the park."

Dog rolls over.

"Let's play ball!" says Pistachio. She bounces his ball on the floor.

Dog snorts. Pistachio opens the door. Dog opens one eye.

"Come on, Dog." Pistachio is growing impatient.

Dog grunts as he heaves himself up onto his tiny legs. He waddles to the door. He looks outside. He sighs, shakes his head, and waddles back to his cushion.

Minutes later, he is snoring like a small train engine. Pistachio rolls her eyes.

Things have got to change around here, she thinks. *Dog will die of boredom.*

The next morning, Pistachio stuffs an astonished Dog into her schoolbag.

"School is sometimes boring too, but you might learn something new," says Pistachio. "Like reading or geography. Wouldn't that be exciting?"

Dog stares at her from the bottom of the schoolbag. He doesn't seem very excited.

Penny, who has been spying on Pistachio from beneath the bed, yells, "Wanna go school wif Dog!"

"Shhhhh, Penny! I'll bring you to school tomorrow," Pistachio lies.

"Wanna go NOW!" Penny roars.

Pistachio hears her mother coming up the stairs. She has to act fast.

"Here, Penny, you can wear my princess crown!"

Penny stops crying. She crawls out from under the bed. She is covered in dustballs.

"Weally?" She puts the crown on. It covers half her face.

"I better be going," says Pistachio as she shoulders her enormous schoolbag.

"What do you have in there?" asks her mother as Pistachio runs down the stairs. "It looks awfully heavy."

"Mr. Grumblebrain gave us a ton of homework," mutters Pistachio. "As usual." She runs out the door.

"Have a good day, princess!" calls her mother.

Rats! Pistachio has forgotten that it's Show and Tell at school today.

First, Chichi presents his favorite paper clip. He shows the class how he can twist it like a pretzel. Mr. Grumblebrain is not impressed.

Then, Fatima, the teacher's pet, presents her butterfly collection. She gives the Latin name to every single one: *Danaus plexippus, Zerene eurydice, Lycaeides melissa melissa*—Most of the students fall asleep.

"Verrrrrry interesting, Miss Fatima," says Mr. Grumblebrain. "Your turn, Miss Pistachio."

Pistachio peeks into her schoolbag. She has no choice. She will have to present her dog for Show and Tell.

"Come on out, Dog," whispers Pistachio. Dog snorts.

"Is someone blowing their nose in your schoolbag?" asks Sebastian. Everybody giggles.

"Dog," says Pistachio. "Wake up!"

Pistachio dumps her schoolbag on Mr. Grumblebrain's desk. Dog flops out like a pile of laundry. He shakes his head. His ears flap like clothes on a line. A stack of exam papers flutter to the floor. Dog sniffs Mr. Grumblebrain's apple and licks it. Then he swallows an eraser in one gulp. He stretches out on the desk and promptly falls asleep again.

By this time, the class is roaring with laughter. Elliot is the first to throw his eraser at the dog. He is not the last.

"Get that hairy beast off my desk!" yells Mr. Grumblebrain. "NOW!"

Pistachio, her face as red as a tomato, stuffs Dog back in her schoolbag, and, head held high, walks to her desk. She sits and stares straight ahead, wishing she were invisible. Or instantly transported to a desert island. Or both.

Chapter 2

The Audition

Two days later, Pistachio is walking back from school with Madeline, her best friend, when she spots a sign posted in the window of the bookstore.

WANTED

Talented, intelligent, beautiful dog to play starring role in a theater production. Only serious dogs need apply. Call 321-B-A-R-K for an audition.

Management, Doggone Theater

Fireworks go off in Pistachio's mind. "That's it!" she cries.

"What are you talking about?" says Madeline.

"Read that," says Pistachio. "That's the perfect job for Dog!"

Madeline reads the sign. At first, she smiles. Then she starts giggling. Then she roars with laughter.

"You've got to be kidding," she gasps, tears streaming down her face.

"What? What's so funny?" asks Pistachio.

"Can't you read?" says Madeline. "It says, 'Wanted…talented, intelligent, beautiful dog.' Hahaha!"

"So?" says Pistachio impatiently.

"Your dog is a fat ball of fur," says Madeline, "with a brain the size of a green pea."

"How can you say that?" shouts
Pistachio, "Dog has many hidden
talents."

"Like snoring?" asks Madeline. "Like
eating erasers? Like sleeping all day?"

"He needs his beauty sleep," says
Pistachio. "And, anyway, you don't
know anything about dogs."

"Pistachio Shoelace!" says Madeline.

"Your dog couldn't ever, ever in a million, trillion years, star in a show. He has nothing between his tiny ears!" And Madeline skips away down the sidewalk.

Pistachio stands there, her cheeks burning like wildfire. "I'll show her," she says. "She'll eat her words."

The next day, Pistachio gets up early and washes and brushes Dog until his fur shines. She dresses him in his best dog collar. The bright purple one. They have a one o'clock audition at the Doggone Theater.

They are not alone. The place is
bursting with dogs and their proud
masters. Some dogs do double-somersaults.
Others juggle balls or shoes. A beagle
balances a teacup on her nose. Two
dachshunds do weird contortions.
They look like wrestling sausages. A
brown terrier tap-dances on a table. A
Chihuahua plays the trumpet.

Pistachio looks at Dog. He is sleeping
soundly at her feet. She sighs.

The dogs and their masters are called in one by one. Finally, it is their turn. Pistachio wakes Dog up and they pass through the small green door and onto the bare stage of a huge theater. The red velvet seats seem to climb up to the roof. Pistachio is blinded by the bright spotlights.

"Please take your places on the stage," says a deep voice that comes from nowhere. Pistachio squints into the dark theater. She can just make out a woman wearing thick glasses and sitting in the front row. She holds a clipboard in her hand. She is the theater director.

"No time to waste," says the woman. "Let's get this over with. I'm exhausted."

"What should we do?" asks Pistachio.

"Isn't it obvious? Go stand on the X and show me what your dog can do."

Pistachio gulps. Dog can't do much except find a ball. And that's only if it is hiding behind his bowl.

She walks to the center of the stage where a big X is chalked on the floor. "Dog, come here," she calls.

"Dog?" she calls again, a bit louder this time. *Where is he?*

The director sighs. "I don't have all day," she says. "You have only one minute left! Let's gogogo!"

"Dog?" whispers Pistachio, as she walks toward the green velvet curtain. "Come on, Dog. This is your big chance!"

Then her heart drops. She can hear Dog snoring away. She pulls the curtain back and there he is, sleeping like a sloth, belly-up, his tiny legs waving in the air.

Pistachio's shoulders droop. "Oooh, Dog," groans Pistachio. She is so disappointed.

The woman stands up. She adjusts her glasses, peers at Dog, and smiles. "Hey! This might be the one!" she exclaims.

"We are looking for a dog to play Sleeping Beauty."

Dog snores loudly.

"Brilliant!" says the director. "He's got the part!"

Pistachio's heart somersaults. She kneels down by Dog and hugs him tightly. "Oh, Dog," she whispers. "You are amazing!"

• Chapter 3 •
Stardom

"What's his name?" asks the director.

"Dog," says Pistachio. "Dog Shoelace."

"That won't do. He needs a stage name. A name for a star!"

She is right, thinks Pistachio. *Dog is going to have an exciting new life, so he needs an exciting new name.*

That evening, Pistachio looks up words in the dictionary. She tries them out on Dog.

"Frederic the Fantastic?" says Pistachio. Dog rolls his eyes.

"Astounding Antonio?" says Pistachio. Dog sighs.

"Stupendous Stirling?" says Pistachio.

Dog puts his head on his paws and closes his eyes.

It is Pistachio's turn to sigh. Then she thinks of her grandfather.

His name is Maurice.

"Maurice?" she whispers. "Maurice the Magnificent?"

Dog smiles in his sleep.

Life becomes a whirlwind for Pistachio and Maurice the Magnificent. There are rehearsals every day

after school. Maurice practices sleeping for hours on end. There are costume fittings. There are appointments with the manicurist, who paints his nails a lovely shade of peony pink, and the *coiffeur*, who curls the hair between his ears. Pistachio and Maurice are interviewed over and over by the press. They want to know every single detail of Maurice's life. When did he start dreaming of being an actor? What is his favorite color? What does he like to eat? Does he have a secret love?

Life is definitely not boring anymore.

Pistachio invites her family and her friends to the opening night. Even Madeline is there. They all sit together in the front row. As soon as the curtains are drawn, the audience falls silent. They are hypnotized by Maurice's performance. No one has ever seen an actor sleep or snore with such flair.

The play is an astounding success. When Maurice comes out to bow, he gets a standing ovation. Only Madeline stays seated.

Maurice the Magnificent is a star!
The show is extended for six months.
Maurice has his own dressing room. It is
filled with flowers and fresh bones.

His fans wait for him every night at

the back door of the theater. Poodles faint. Beagles throw kibble at him. His face is on the first page of every newspaper in the country.

Pistachio is so proud. All she can talk about is Maurice…*Maurice did this, Maurice did that, Maurice is…*

"That's enough! Stop talking about Maurice!" says Madeline one day. "I can't stand it anymore!"

Pistachio sniffs. "You're just totally jealous, Madeline Maplehead! You desperately wish you had a wonderful world-famous dog like Maurice!"

"Jealous," says Madeline, "of a fat furball? You must be kidding." She snickers loudly and walks away. As soon as Madeline turns the corner, she frowns and her shoulders droop. She looks like she has lost something precious.

· Chapter 4 ·
Dognapping

But then, one terrible day, Pistachio goes backstage to Maurice's dressing room after the show.

"Maurice!" calls Pistachio. "It is time to go home." She enters the dressing room. It is empty. A ruby dog collar lies on the floor. A half-chewed bone is abandoned on a cushion.

Suddenly, Pistachio's throat is as dry as sandpaper. She knows something is wrong.

"Maurice!" she cries. "Where are you?" She looks under the couch. In the top drawer of the dresser. In the closet. Then she sees the note taped to the mirror.

Pistachio's heart stands still. Maurice has been dognapped!

As Pistachio slowly walks home, her mind is racing. *What should I do? If I call the police, the dognapper might hurt Maurice. Should I pay the ransom? What if the dognapper keeps Maurice a prisoner forever?*

Suddenly, Pistachio sees Madeline swinging like a monkey from a tree branch. She seems to be waiting for Pistachio.

"So, where is the world-famous furball?" asks Madeline, "Did he fall off the stage?"

Pistachio tells her the whole, terrible story. She is almost in tears.

"What should I do, Madeline? You are my best friend. Please help me."

"Why would I want to help you?" Madeline asks. "I don't feel like I am your best friend anymore."

Madeline swings back and forth. Pistachio walks away.

Pistachio makes up her mind. She
will trick the dognapper. She will save
Maurice.

That night at nine o'clock, Pistachio
sneaks out of the house. She runs all the
way to the park. She places an envelope
at the foot of the chestnut tree. Then
she looks around to make sure that no
one is there. She scrambles up the tree
and settles on a big branch. An owl
hoots and sails off into the dark velvet
night. Pistachio waits. She doesn't move
an inch.

At exactly ten o'clock, a shadow creeps silently toward the foot of the tree. Pistachio holds her breath.

The shadow grabs the envelope and snickers. Pistachio jumps down from the branch. She lands on the shadow. The shadow shrieks. Pistachio shines her flashlight in the shadow's face.

"Madeline?" cries Pistachio. "*You* are the dognapper?"

Just then, a fat, furry ball flies into Pistachio's arms and nearly licks her face off.

"Why did you steal Maurice?" asks Pistachio.

"You were right," answers Madeline miserably. "I *was* jealous. Terribly jealous. I wanted to be your best friend again. You only had eyes for Maurice. I felt so lonely. I'm sorry."

Pistachio is silent for a moment. Had she really forgotten all about her friend? Maybe she had.

"How about if the three of us become best friends?" says Pistachio. "You, Maurice, and I."

"Okay," says Madeline. "But can you and Maurice get off of me first? You are both pretty heavy."

Maurice the Magnificent decided that he had had enough excitement and that it was time to retire. He needed to catch up on his sleep.

Pistachio and Madeline went on to start a school for dog-actors.

Dog Stars!
Do you want your dog to become a star?
Does your dog have any talent?
Find out at Dog Stars!
Call Madeline or Pistachio
444-STAR